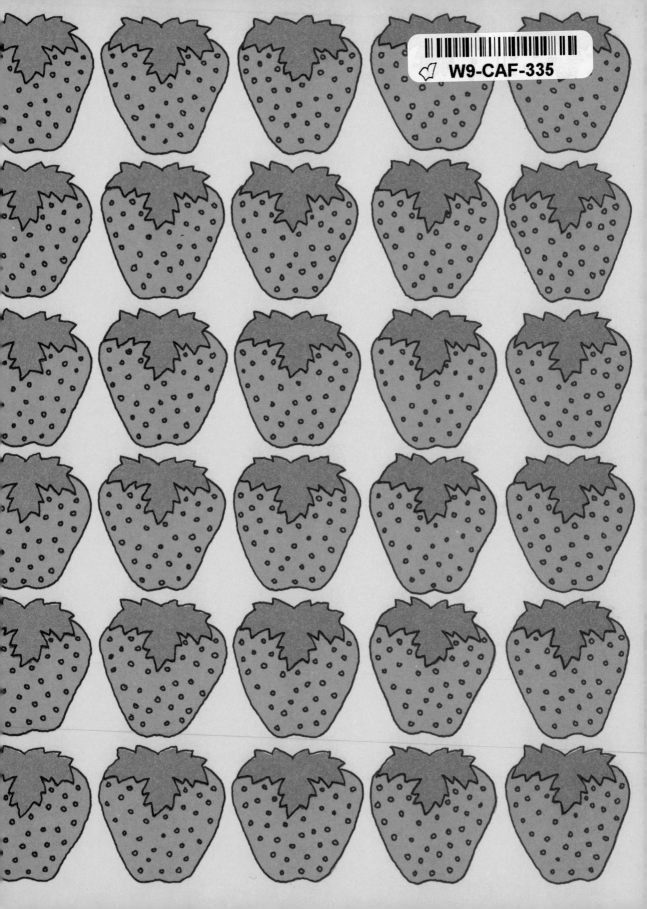

this
strawberry book
belongs to

Megan
Cook

*this book
is for
the
chicken
who likes
bears*

Library of Congress Catalog Card Number: 75-3807
ISBN: Trade 0-88470-014-3, Library 0-88470-015-1

Weekly Reader Books' Edition

the strawberry book of
colors
by Richard Hefter

ACME PAINTING CO.

a strawberry book ®

Jack, Max and Axle are the best painters at the Acme Painting Company.

Jack paints things yellow.
He loves yellow.
Jack is a very fast painter.

Max paints things blue.
He is crazy about blue.
Max is a very careful painter.

Axle paints things red.
He adores red.
Axle is a very quick painter.

Jack is painting the wall yellow.
Max is painting the ceiling blue.
Oops.

Yellow and blue make green.
Jack and Max make a mess.

Jack is up
on a scaffold.
Axle is
underneath.
Look out Axle!

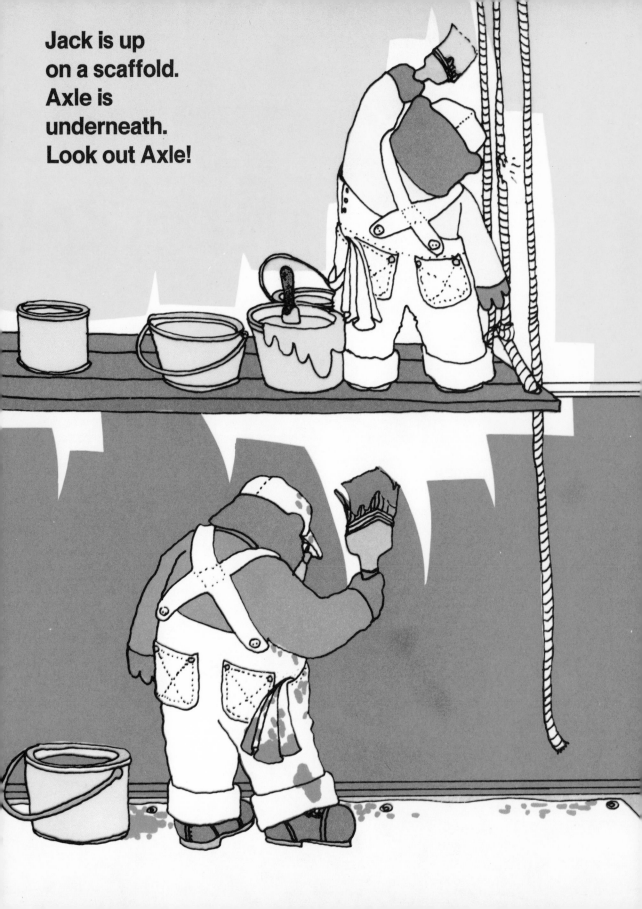

Yellow and red make orange.
Paint on his head makes Axle mad.

Max is on a ladder.
Axle is on another ladder.

Crunch! Crash!
Blue and red make purple.

There goes Jack
with his yellow paint.

Here comes Max with his blue paint.

Away goes Axle with his red paint.

**Jack, Max and Axle
are painting a rainbow on Margaret's house.**

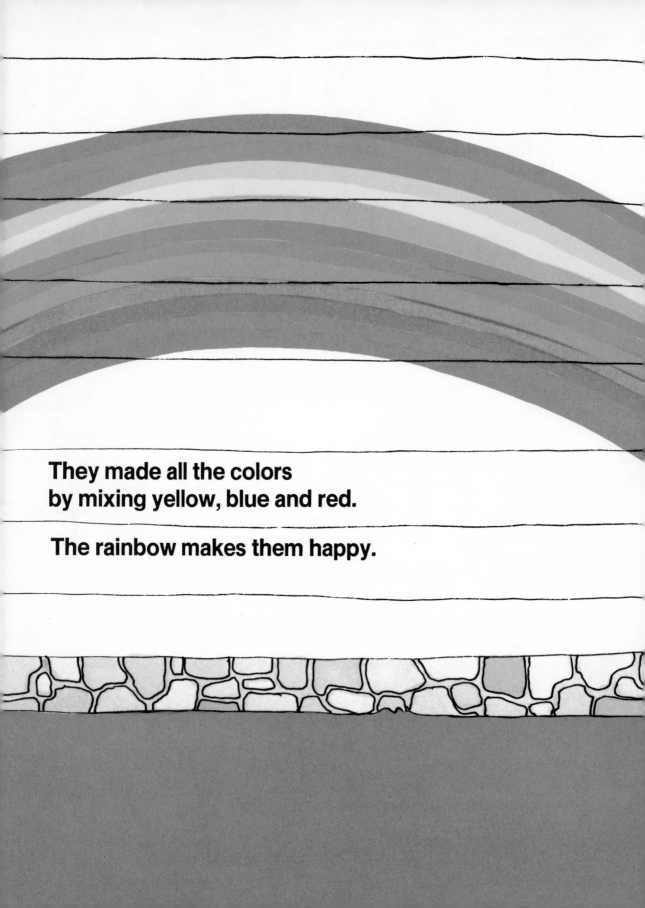

They made all the colors
by mixing yellow, blue and red.

The rainbow makes them happy.

**Margaret isn't happy,
she wanted her house painted white.**

**Jack, Max and Axle can mix
almost any color they want
with yellow, blue and red.**

They are the best painters
at the Acme Painting Company.

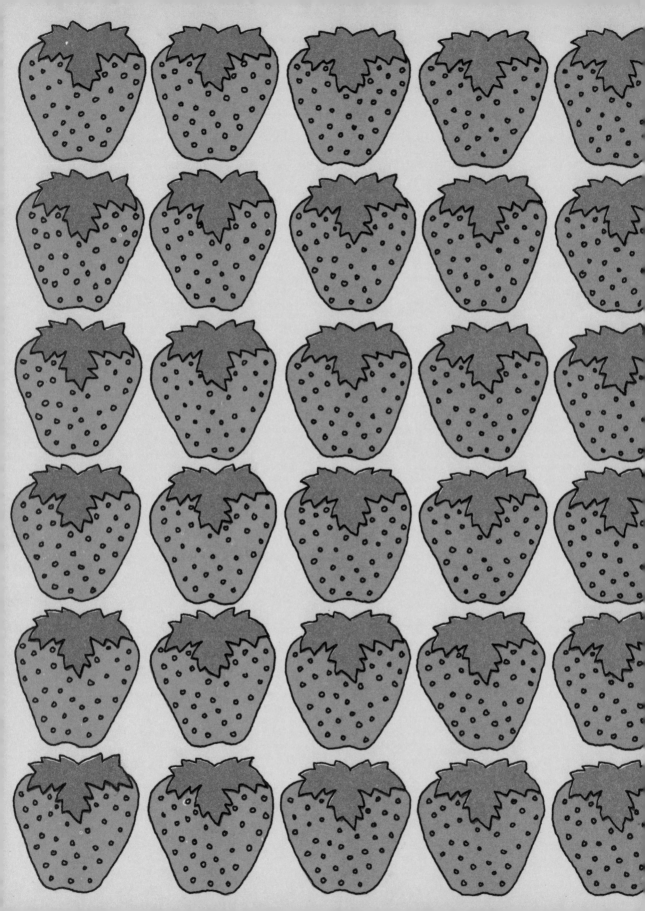